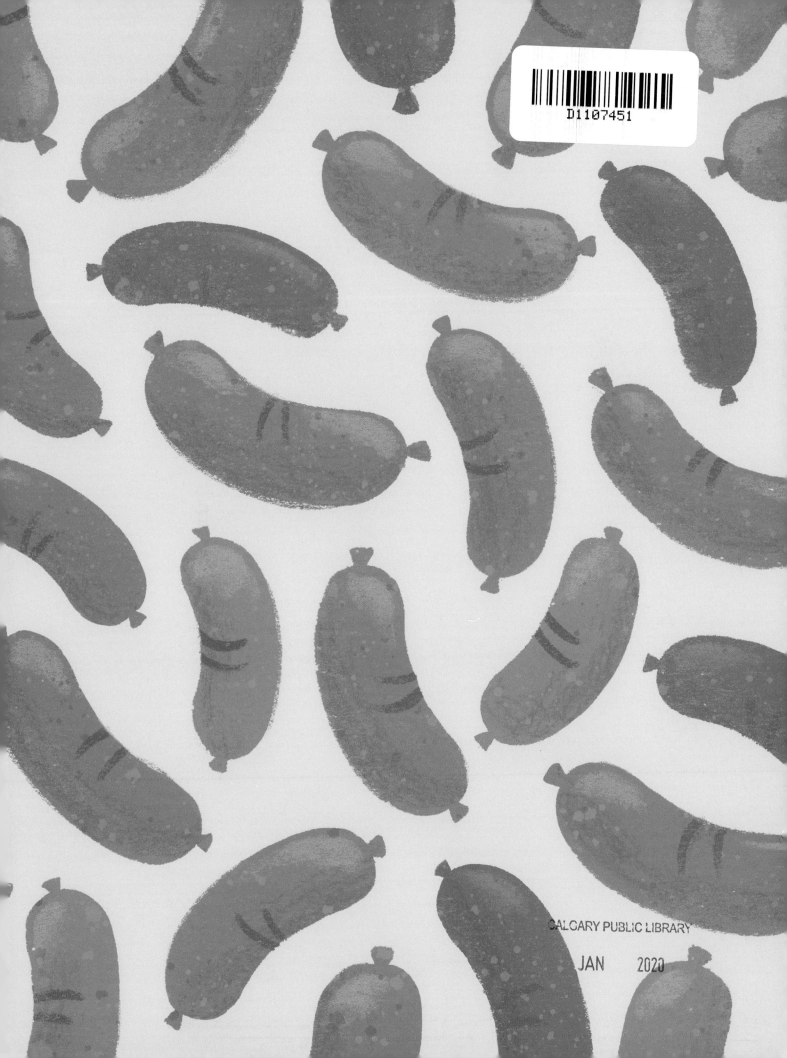

For Vinaya, thank you for putting
up with me on my Gus days.

First published 2019 by Macmillan Children's Books
an imprint of Pan Macmillan
20 New Wharf Road, London N1 9RR
Associated companies throughout the world
www.panmacmillan.com

ISBN 978-1-5098-5434-9 (HB)
ISBN 978-1-5098-5435-6 (PB)

1 3 5 7 9 8 6 4 2

A CIP catalogue record for this book is available
from the British Library.

Printed in China

THIS IS
GUS

Chris Chatterton

This is Gus.

Gus doesn't like
much of anything.

Gus doesn't like being petted.

Gus doesn't like going for walks.

He doesn't like fetching sticks or balls.

And he certainly doesn't like
making new friends.

Gus doesn't like birthdays either.

He doesn't like cake.
He doesn't like balloons.
He doesn't like presents.

That was until I arrived.
Now Gus *loves* birthdays.

He likes bathtime.

He likes hide-and-seek.

And he really likes hugs.

Almost as much as he likes . . .

...SAUSAGES!

He likes the smell of sausages.

He likes the shape of sausages.

But most of all, he likes
the taste of sausages.

And he isn't the only one.

But Gus absolutely, definitely
doesn't like to share.

Sometimes I think Gus
doesn't like *anything* . . .

. . . except sausages . . .

. . . and me.

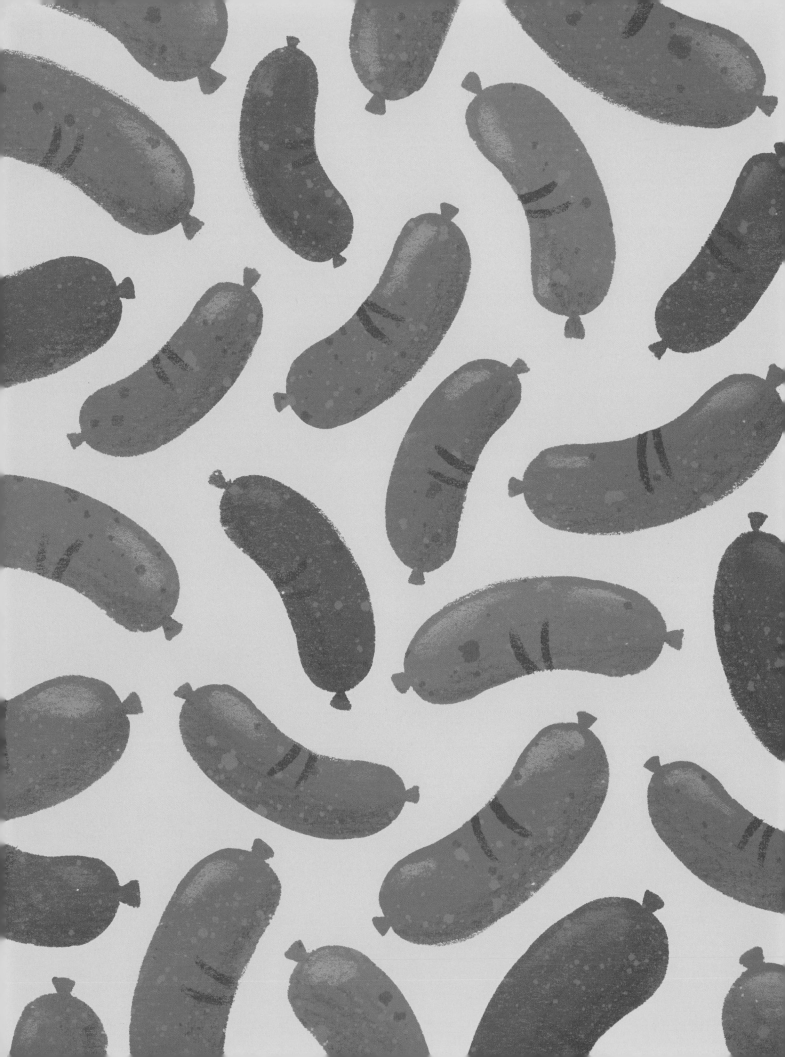